Do you want to bet?

"Chris doesn't like me," I objected.

"He does, too, Darlene," said Lauren. "Don't you know? We've got a bet going. Becky's friends said that he'd invite her out first. We said that it would be you."

"You bet on who he's going to date first?" I practically shouted at her.

"Shh!" said Lauren, giggling. "I wasn't supposed to tell you."

"I've never had a date," I said, exasperated. "And I'll be darned if my first date is going to be to win a bet for you guys."

**Look for these and other books
in THE GYMNASTS series:**

THE GYMNASTS

#13 FIRST DATE

Elizabeth Levy

AN
APPLE
PAPERBACK

SCHOLASTIC INC.
New York Toronto London Auckland Sydney

ISBN 0-590-42825-X

12 11 10 9 8 7 6 5 4 3 2 1   0 1 2 3 4 5/9

Printed in the U.S.A.   28

First Scholastic printing, September 1990

To George, on our first date

FIRST DATE

Is He Cute or What?

Our gym is not exactly high tech. We don't have foam pits or any of the fancy new equipment I see in the gymnastics magazines. So when we get a new piece of equipment, it's good news.

"Darlene, did you see that new hunk?" asked Becky Dyson, who was standing next to me. The two of us had gotten out of school early because of a teachers' conference. We had come straight to the gym before the rest of our teams. The boys' team was already working out.

"It's a harness, not a hunk," I said to her. I was surprised. Becky Dyson is an incredibly good gymnast, much better than I am. She should have recognized the harness contraption that Patrick had rigged up over the trampoline.

It's a training device for learning complicated new tricks without hurting yourself.

"I'm really excited," I said. "I've always wanted to try out a harness. We can practice double flips. It'll be fun."

"Darlene," said Becky, "you've been with the Pinecones too long. It's time to get back into the real world. I wasn't talking about the harness. I was talking about the hunk about to get into it. Is he cute or what?"

Becky pointed to a new boy who was standing next to Patrick. He had a tan face, but his arms and legs were pale. The contrast made him look a little funny, but he was very muscular. He was taller than the other boys, with hair long enough so that he had to push it out of his eyes with a sweatband.

"I'm more interested in the new harness," I said.

"Darlene, you're sick," said Becky, running her fingers through her blonde hair. "I tell you, thirteen is too old to be hanging around with the Pinecones. I think they're affecting your hormones."

"Give me a break," I begged her. "Leave my hormones out of it."

Becky and I go to the same school, and we work out at the same gym, the Evergreen Gymnastics Academy, with our coach Patrick Harmon. Naturally people think Becky and I have everything in common.

People can be *so* wrong. Becky and I couldn't be more different. She's white. I'm black. She's a great athlete and an incredibly competitive gymnast. I'm good, but I don't think I'll ever be great.

Most important, I'm a Pinecone. She's not. Becky would say she's the lucky one. The Pinecones are my team. Becky is on the advanced team. We don't win as many competitions as Becky's team. Let's be honest: We don't win many competitions, period. At thirteen, I'm the oldest Pinecone. I like the fact that my friends on the Pinecones aren't boy crazy the way the girls at school are.

Patrick saw us staring at the new contraption. He waved to us to come over to the trampoline.

"Becky, Darlene," he shouted, "come meet our newest addition."

"Remember, I saw him first," whispered Becky, "so hands off."

"Becky, you haven't even met him yet. Maybe he's a nerd."

"If he's a nerd, then I'm a Pinecone," said Becky. She winked at me. "And I'm *not* a Pinecone."

Thank goodness for that, I said to myself.

We walked over to where the boys' team was

standing around the trampoline with the harness.

"Patrick finally sprang for some new equipment," said Jared Jockett. Jared is my idea of kind-of cute. He's got red hair and freckles, and wears glasses. He's very sweet. He's the brother of Cindi, one of my best friends on the Pinecones. The Pinecones all think that Jared has a crush on me, but so far I haven't really seen any sign of it.

"Hi, Patrick," I said. "This looks neat. Are the girls going to get to use this, too?" I was only half teasing. Our gym used to be all girls. I'd liked it that way. Patrick gave us his total attention. Then we got a boys' team.

Patrick grinned at me. "Darlene," he said, "what do you take me for? Of course the Pinecones and all the other girls are going to use the new harness. I just want you to see what a real expert does. Darlene and Becky, meet Christopher Ferguson. He's going to work out at our gym with us this year. Chris is a freestyle skier."

"Hi, Chris," gushed Becky. "Do you mean that incredibly dangerous skiing where you go off the jump and turn somersaults in the air? I've seen that on television. I never thought I'd get to meet anybody who actually had the nerve to do it. . . ."

Chris laughed. He seemed to try to catch my eye. I'm sure he was used to girls making a big

4

deal about him all the time. He looked like he was about sixteen years old. He had bright blue eyes that were hard not to look at, especially because his face was so deeply tanned.

"It's not so dangerous," said Chris.

"You've got to be a gymnast to do those tricks on skis," said Patrick. "In fact, Chris was telling me that most freestyle skiers study gymnastics. He needs to sharpen his skills so he can do more complicated tricks."

"My sister's the real gymnast in the family. She has to live in California because she works out with the Supertwisters team. She's got a real chance for the next Olympics. I started late and need to catch up. That's why I'm taking gymnastics here."

"Chris, why don't you show them what you can do?" suggested Patrick.

Chris jumped up on the trampoline. The ropes and wires from the harness were attached to the ceiling, and the harness clipped around his waist, so that with Patrick's help he could be suspended over the trampoline.

Patrick took hold of the pulleys on the side where he could regulate the tension.

"Okay, Chris. Let 'er rip," said Patrick. Chris jumped until he was easily reaching six feet above the trampoline. When I jump on the trampoline I'm lucky if I can get four feet into the air.

"Try an Arabian somersault," said Patrick. An Arabian somersault is a full twist in a layout position with a pike just at the peak.

Chris jumped higher and higher. Then he put his hands over his head, twisted his body in a complete circle, and flung his legs over his head. He came down, lightly touched the trampoline, and did it again — if anything, more perfectly than before.

"Awesome!" I heard gasps from behind me. It was Lauren, Jodi, Cindi, Ti An, and Ashley. The Pinecones had all arrived, and they were watching Chris as if he were a Greek god who had suddenly descended on our gym.

I watched Chris do the trick again. He was awesome, all right. My teammates were all looking up at him with the same expression. It wasn't one that I liked. I had seen it too many times before.

My dad is a pro football player with the Denver Broncos. I've grown up with people worshiping my father just because he's a professional athlete. I've seen people hanging around football practice, convinced that they're watching something superhuman. Well, I'm not in awe of super athletes. And I wasn't sure I wanted one in my gym.

First Impressions Aren't Wrong

"Who is that guy?" asked Jodi.

"Superman," said Lauren. "Can't you see? He flies through the air."

"He is *seriously* good," said Jodi.

"And I saw him first," said Becky. "So you Pinecones kindly take your grubby faces elsewhere. He doesn't want a whole fan club."

"Is he joining the boys' team?" asked Jodi. "My mom will love that. He looks like he belongs in the Olympics."

Jodi's mom coaches the boys' team. She was a champion gymnast in her day. And so was Jodi's father. Jodi pretends that she doesn't care that she herself isn't a top-grade athlete, but I'm not so sure. I think Jodi may be hiding that she *does* mind. It's tough coming from a family of world-class athletes. I know all about that. Dad is such a superstar that when people hear I'm a gymnast, they just assume that I'm an Olympic star.

"He's not officially joining our team," said Jared. "He's just working out here. He's a skier, not a gymnast."

Chris did a double flip in the air. His body was perfectly aligned, his shoulders square to his hips. "If he ever wanted to be a gymnast, he'd be super," said Lauren.

"Can you believe that guy is my age!" exclaimed Jared. "Talk about depressing!"

"You're kidding!" said Becky, sounding disappointed. "He's only thirteen? I thought he was sixteen."

"What's the matter, Becky?" teased Jared. "You only interested in older guys?"

"Well, he looks older than you," said Becky.

When Jared first came to the gym, Becky acted all interested in him and his friend Ryan. As soon as she realized Jared wasn't at all interested in her, she dropped him as if he were a big zero. That just made me like Jared all the more.

Chris put his hands on the edge of the trampoline and did a somersault onto the ground, somehow managing to do it without tangling up the lines from the pulley.

He slipped off the harness.

"Did Patrick get the harness just for him?" I asked.

Jared shook his head. "Are you kidding? Chris's family donated it to Patrick's gym. Apparently both his parents are sports nuts, but Chris is having trouble at school because he was spending so much time at Lake Placid in New York learning to freestyle. His parents want him home more. And he lives just about two blocks from here. In fact, he lives in your neighborhood. Haven't you ever seen him before?"

I shook my head. "How did you learn all this about him so fast?" I asked.

"Easy," said Jared. "Chris told me. Chris does a lot of talking." Jared sounded as if he didn't like Chris. I didn't blame him. It must have been a shock for a new guy to show up who was not on your team, but who was a champion athlete whose parents pushed their weight around by donating equipment to the gym.

I wouldn't like it if it happened to us Pinecones. I thought Chris was probably an arrogant kid.

Chris handed the harness to Patrick. "Thanks," Chris said. "This is going to work out great for me."

"It's going to work out for all of us," said Patrick. "You'll be working mostly with Sarah Josephson on your tumbling moves. I'll help on the harness. Sarah's strong, but you're a little big for her to do the counterweights all alone."

Jodi's mom was late getting to the gym. "Sarah Josephson," muttered Jodi. "Do you think I'll ever get used to having a last name that's different than my mom's?" Jodi's mom had recently remarried, and Jodi still isn't the happiest kid in the world about it.

"Your mom's going to have a great time working with Chris," I said. "You have to admit he's pretty good."

"And cute," added Lauren. I stared at her. "Well, he is," she said.

I wondered if Chris had overheard Lauren. He looked our way, and he kind of half winked at us. It was a conceited wink.

Then he turned to Patrick. "I thought I'd be working with you," said Chris. "Didn't my parents pay for private lessons with you?" He sounded petulant. But Patrick was *our* coach. He wasn't going to have time always to be working with this new kid, no matter how good he was.

"You'll get private lessons with me," said Patrick, "and you'll take the group workouts with Sarah."

"I've never had a woman coach before," said Chris.

"Chris," warned Patrick, "you're only thirteen.

If you plan on even *living* until the twenty-first century, you'd better drop that attitude. Sarah Josephson is one of the best gymnastics coaches you could hope to work with."

"And she's my mom," blurted out Jodi. "Say anything nasty about her, and you'll have to deal with me."

Chris at least had the good grace to blush — even through his tan.

I don't usually make snap judgments about people. Usually I'm pretty tolerant. But my first impressions about people are usually right. There was something about Chris that I just didn't like.

3

9.9 for Fluttering Eyelashes

"Oh, Chris," said Becky, just as we were about to break into our separate groups.

"Yes?" said Chris. He had been about to walk away with the other boys.

"Maybe . . ." Becky paused. I couldn't believe it. She actually fluttered her eyelashes up and down. Unfortunately Becky's got practically colorless eyelashes, and she didn't have much to flutter. She looked kind of silly.

"Do you have something in your eye?" Chris asked.

"Uh . . . no," said Becky. "I was just wondering if I could try the harness."

"I think you'd better ask Patrick," said Chris. "He's in charge of it, not me."

"Patrick! Patrick!" shrieked Becky. "Can I try the harness, pul-leese?"

"Sure," said Patrick.

"Watch this," I muttered to Jodi. "The great performer takes the stage."

"I kind of liked her performance with her eyelashes," said Jodi with a giggle.

"Yeah," I said. "A 9.9 for Becky Dyson on the eyelashes."

Cindi cracked up. She was laughing so hard that Chris turned to look at us. Cindi's got a weird laugh.

Becky casually put the harness between her legs and under her arms. "They had one of these when I went to gymnastics camp," she said. "We've needed one for a long time. Chris, we'll never be able to thank your family enough. Patrick keeps us in the Dark Ages as far as anything new goes."

"Becky," said Patrick, dryly, "suppose you stop complaining about the old equipment in the gym and show us what you can do with the new."

Becky jumped up and down, getting a rhythm going on the trampoline. The trampoline creaked and groaned as she gathered more and more momentum.

"I want to try a double flip," shouted Becky.

"Just do a forward somersault at first," said Patrick. "I want to make sure that you're comfortable with the harness."

Becky tucked her legs underneath her. Patrick pulled down on the pulley controlling the harness, giving her extra height. She swung through the air as if she were weightless. It looked so easy. I *had* to try it.

"This is great," screamed Becky. "Chris, what was that move *you* were doing? I want to try it."

"It was an Arabian," said Chris. He stood next to me.

"Your friend is good," he said.

Lauren giggled at the word "friend."

"Did I say something funny?" Chris asked, not taking his eyes off Becky. I didn't blame him for being impressed with her.

He couldn't stop watching her. I couldn't, either. Becky was really, really good. She looked even more impressive in the harness, as if no trick was too hard for her. She kept her toes pointed and her body tight. She twisted and turned in the air, going higher and higher with each rebound.

"Are you and she on the same team?" Chris asked me.

"Us? No!" I choked out. "Why would you think that?"

"You and she look like two of the older girls here," said Chris. "I saw you come in together. I figured you must be on the same team."

"We're not," I said sharply.

"Oh," said Chris. "Sorry. Maybe you're in a more advanced group. My sister makes . . . what's that girl's name?" Chris pointed to Becky.

"Becky," I reminded him.

"Yeah, my sister makes Becky look like an amateur."

Lauren's eyes opened wide. "Your sister's got to be Heidi Ferguson, the gymnast!"

"Yeah," said Chris.

"I can't believe it!" exclaimed Lauren. "I read that she was originally from Denver, but I thought you all lived in California."

"No, just Heidi," said Chris. "She trains with the Supertwisters Club out there." Chris looked uncomfortable with all the talk about his sister. He changed the subject. "So *are* you?" he asked me.

It was hard for me to make much sense of what he was saying. "Am I what?" I asked him, a little annoyed.

"In a more advanced group than Becky?"

At that Lauren couldn't control herself anymore. She burst out laughing.

"Darlene . . . she's a Pinecone," said Lauren.

Chris stopped watching Becky. "What's a Pine-cone?" he asked.

"A member of the world's most incredible team," said Cindi.

Jared guffawed.

"What are you laughing at, creep?" Cindi asked her brother.

"Nothing. Who comes to every Pinecone meet and cheers?" asked Jared.

"You do," I said, sticking up for him.

"Right," said Jared. "I just don't think you should lie to poor Chris and tell him that the Pinecones are the best team in the gym."

"We are in spirit," I said. "We're the best of friends, and that's what counts, not winning meets."

"My sister would never agree with you," said Chris.

"Who cares?" I said, a little more sharply than I expected. I didn't like this guy bragging about his sister. It annoyed me. I watched Becky bouncing up and down on the trampoline, and I knew that I could never do what she was doing. It hadn't bothered me before that Becky was so much better than me, but now it did.

Strengths and Weaknesses

Finally we broke up into our own groups to begin our workout. Unfortunately the Pinecones couldn't stop talking about Chris as we warmed up.

"Hey, Patrick," Cindi called across the gym. "Did you know that Chris's sister is Heidi Ferguson?"

"Of course Patrick must know," said Ashley. "Heidi Ferguson is *so* famous."

"Yeah, well, if she's so famous, how come I didn't know she was from Denver?" asked Jodi.

"It's because she trains in California, dodo," said Ashley. "Don't you ever read anything in the gymnastics magazines?"

"Girls," said Patrick, "I know it's exciting to

have Chris training with us. And, yes, Cindi, I did know that Heidi is Chris's sister, but she's in California, and we have ourselves to worry about."

"But wouldn't you like to coach her?" asked Ti An. "I saw her on television. She was awesome."

"Awesome's the right name for the Fergusons," said Patrick. "Chris and Heidi's mom was a world-class skier in the 1950s."

"Hey, Darlene, you'll have something in common to talk about when you go out," teased Jodi.

"What are you talking about?" I asked.

"You can talk about growing up with a famous athlete in the house," teased Jodi, ". . . on your first date. I saw the way that guy was looking at you. He liked you."

"Jodi, please," I begged her. "He liked Becky."

"I don't think so," said Cindi with a giggle. "I think Becky liked *him*, but he liked you."

Patrick shook his head. "Girls, girls," he said, "let's cut the gossip and do a little gymnastics."

"That's fine with me," I said. "I *hate* gossip."

"I think it's fun," said Jodi. "I think you and Chris would be cute together."

"Give me a break," I groaned.

"I agree," said Patrick. "That's enough of that kind of talk, Jodi. I don't like gossip in my gym. And Darlene hasn't even done anything to deserve it."

18

Patrick was more right than he knew. A lot of my friends started having "boyfriends" when they were ten or eleven, but I always thought that was silly. Mom and Dad told me that I couldn't even *think* about dating until I was thirteen. So now I'm thirteen and an "official" teenager. I still haven't gone on a date. It doesn't bother me. It's just that the Pinecones seem to fantasize that I have this terrific social life, when in reality it's a big zero. I looked across the room to where the boys were working out. Chris was hanging in an iron cross from the rings. He was suspended in midair, pushing the rings out to their fullest extension and supporting all his weight with his arms and shoulders. His arms were shaking from the effort.

"Oh, Darlene," said Patrick, "as long as I'm defending you, would you mind giving me your attention?"

"Uh, sorry," I mumbled.

Patrick grinned. "I know we have a big distraction today, but I'm hoping you girls will get used to him."

Lauren tittered.

"Pinecones, I'm serious," said Patrick. "We have two months to prepare for our next meet season. I think it's time for each of you to move up a notch. I want you all to think about your own strengths and weaknesses. I won't make decisions for you. I want *you* to tell me what two events you want to concentrate on."

"Easy for me," said Lauren. "The vault." Lauren is built like a powerhouse. She's not very tall, but she's strong, and vault is her best event. It's my worst.

"I guess I like floor the best," said Ti An. "Or maybe bars, no, maybe beam . . . and I don't hate vault." Ti An looked confused. "It's hard to choose."

"Maybe it's because you're not really great at any," said Ashley.

Cindi winked at me. "Good old Ashley," she said. "You're best at the catty event."

Patrick held up his hands. "Girls, don't blurt out the first thing that comes into your head. Take some time with your answers — write them down. Then we'll talk about them together."

"This is beginning to sound like school," grumbled Jodi. "Next, you'll be telling us that we're going to 'share' them out loud."

Patrick laughed. "No, Jodi. First of all, I don't care about spelling or anything like that . . . and we're not going to share them. This will be private. Don't even talk to each other about your strengths and weaknesses. I want your own opinions."

"Becky's good at every event," said Ashley. "I want to be more like Becky."

"Ashley," said Patrick, "I'm not talking about Becky, although even she is not equally good at all events."

Ashley is a bit of a twerp. Sometimes we Pinecones think that Ashley is Becky's revenge on us for all being good friends. Ashley's only nine, and she's an excellent gymnast. It's just that Ashley's got her values screwed up. She really thinks that Becky is perfect, and that there's something wrong with the Pinecones. Every once in a while, Ashley lets her guard down and is a teeny-weeny bit nice. Then she acts as if being nice is all wrong, and she acts mean again. Luckily she's the only one of the Pinecones who is like that. The rest of them are great.

Ti An Truong is just nine. She's as good a gymnast as Ashley, but she lacks the confidence to be really great. Every once in a while, she'll do a move that's just brilliant, and then she'll lose it. But she's getting better. During our last meet, she really turned it on during the floor exercise and saved the day for us.

Cindi Jockett is probably our most consistent gymnast. She's good at almost every event. "Boring," Cindi would probably say. "The only thing flaming about me is my hair," she complains. She's got beautiful bright red hair, just like her brother. Her problem is that she thinks being normal and nice is boring. It isn't.

Jodi Sutton is probably my best friend of the Pinecones. Jodi and I are as different-looking as Becky and I. Jodi's blonde, and her looks hide what she's really like inside. People buy the cliché that pretty blonde girls are airheads. Jodi's much more complicated than that. She's got a temper, but she's incredibly loyal. Once Jodi decides that she's your friend, she's like a pit bull against anybody who does you wrong. Sometimes I tell Jodi to cool it when Becky baits us. Jodi doesn't know the meaning of the phrase "cool it."

It was funny — Patrick asked us to think about our strengths and weaknesses as *gymnasts*, and I immediately thought of our strengths and weaknesses as *kids*. The one thing I've learned as a gymnast is that the thing that messes me up on the balance beam is often the same thing that messes me up in school or with my friends.

From the outside, I look good. The Pinecones tease me that I care too much about clothes and hairstyles. They don't realize that I always feel that I *have* to look good. My dad doesn't. He's expected to look scruffy and tough like a football player, but Mom used to be a model, and she *always* looks good when we're out in public. The newspapers and TV expect Big Beef's wife and daughters to look cute — all the time. I'm not really resentful. I appreciate that Dad's being a football star has brought us the good life. Mom sometimes says that being the wife of a football star is like living in a goldfish bowl. I don't think it's like that at all.

Nobody really stares at goldfish. They're kind of soothing and just there. You take one glance at a goldfish, and that's it. But being the daughter of a celebrity, I feel like everybody's *always* watching me.

When I was ten I realized that I had two choices. I could feel like a freak, or I could let them watch me on my terms. I wouldn't let my guard down. It's one of my strengths. I don't like to do *anything* that I can't control. It's hard to be a really great gymnast and stay in control all the time. I'd have to tell Patrick that my strengths and weaknesses were the same thing.

5

Harness or Booby Trap?

"Okay, Pinecones," said Patrick, the next week. "I've blocked out time for you to practice with the harness. I want to work on some complicated tumbling moves."

"What if I've already written that hanging upside down is not one of my strengths?" asked Lauren. Lauren sometimes gets carsick, and she's the only one of the Pinecones who can get a little bit nauseated if we have to do too many dive rolls in a row.

"I like to hang upside down," said Ti An seriously.

"Maybe you're part bat," joked Lauren. She grinned to show Ti An she was only teasing. "But I'm not."

"Ti An, the vampire!" said Ashley.

Ti An looked hurt. She could take teasing from Lauren, but it was much harder to take from Ashley. Ashley had an edge to her teasing that was missing from Lauren's.

"If there's any Pinecone that's a vampire," said Cindi, "Ashley, you're the one. You should put down as your one strength: 'Have teeth — will bite.' "

Patrick looked annoyed. "Pinecones, no sniping. Let's save some energy for gymnastics. Darlene, why don't you try the harness first?"

"Why am *I* the guinea pig?" I asked.

"You're the oldest. You're the captain," said Patrick. "Show them how it's done."

"I've used the harness before," bragged Ashley. "We had one at the gymnastics camp I went to this summer. It was the same one that Becky went to."

"Then you can be next," said Patrick. He winked at me. Patrick tries to be impartial, but he's got as little patience with Ashley's foolishness as any of us.

Patrick blew a whistle. All the other gymnasts in the gym stopped what they were doing and stared at us.

"Why did you do that?" I hissed at Patrick.

"I want to demonstrate safety procedures," said Patrick. "I want everybody to watch."

"It's a little late to ask me!" I said to him. "I thought I was just going to practice in front of the Pinecones."

"Darlene," said Patrick, "I'm not asking you to perform on national television. This is just for the teams that are here."

"That means Becky's team, the boys' team . . ." I groaned.

"Go for it, Darlene," said Cindi. "You'll show them that the Pinecones have class."

"What do you want, Patrick?" asked Becky.

"I want to demonstrate the safety procedures for the harness," explained Patrick.

"Fine," said Becky, stepping forward to get on the trampoline.

"Not so fast," I said, putting a hand on Becky's arm. "Patrick asked me to show people how." I might not want to be the center of attention, but I wasn't going to let Becky just walk right over me.

"Okay, boys and girls," said Patrick. "Someday, I will be able to have a foam pit here for you to use, but until then, the harness is going to let you do many repetitions of a trick without having to suffer the pain and risk of mistakes."

"Great," I grumbled. "Four of my favorite words: mistakes, suffer, pain, and risk."

Patrick spread his arms wide. "Look, Darlene, we all know that gymnasts have to take risks. As

26

a gymnast you're in an unusual situation as an athlete. You've got to perform some very complex skills, but practicing them is difficult. Every athlete knows that repetition is the only way to improve consistency. In gymnastics, repeating a new move may be dangerous, because each time you make a mistake it can hurt."

"Thanks very much for the confidence lecture," I said.

"Well, think about it," said Patrick. "A typical tennis player might practice a serve three hundred times in one session. She can see her mistakes by the way the ball hits the net or goes out of bounds. But a gymnast can't do a double somersault three hundred times."

Becky giggled. "Darlene — doing a double somersault — even once!"

"Becky, button your lip," said Patrick. "The harness gives you a chance to practice skills that you aren't quite ready to practice alone."

I groaned. "This is the wrong lecture to give to somebody who hates to make mistakes," I said.

Jared and his best friend, Ryan, giggled, but I wasn't trying to be funny.

"All right," said Patrick. "First, it is your responsibility to make sure that the crash mats have been placed properly — not just under the trampoline, but extending two feet in each direction."

"Yeah, we don't want Darlene falling on her head," joked Jodi.

I sighed. "Patrick, maybe I shouldn't be the one to demonstrate this," I said.

"Nonsense," said Patrick. "You're exactly the one I want. Nobody should get into the harness unless there is an adult supervising. There's just too much chance of you getting hurt. The pulleys are controlled by a counterweight, and you have to know what you're doing to operate them. Darlene, slip into the harness."

I did *not* like being the guinea pig.

I put my hands on the safety pad around the frame of the trampoline and did a front somersault across the springs onto the main pad.

I put on the harness. It felt fine and comfortable.

"Okay, jump up and down," said Patrick. "Give me a chance to get into your rhythm."

I was used to jumping up and down on the trampoline, but this time, at the height of my jump, Patrick pulled down on the pulley, causing me to stay suspended up in the air.

"This is fun," I yelled down to Patrick, waving my legs in the air. "I'm flying!" I sang out, pretending that I was Peter Pan.

"Push down again," said Patrick. "I want you to try a front somersault at the height of your next jump."

I pointed my toes and let myself sink onto the trampoline, bounding back up. This time, at the height of my jump, Patrick pulled sharply on the pulley.

"Tuck!" Patrick yelled. I tucked my legs underneath me and started to do a somersault. I was up so much higher than I was used to. I turned upside down and unfortunately chose that moment to look down. I saw all those faces staring up at me, and I froze.

I turned a completely uncontrolled somersault and hung upside down in the harness. I waved my arms, like a whirligig gone mad.

"Relax!" Patrick commanded me. Yelling at somebody to relax when she's dangling upside down doesn't help. I stuck my right leg out, not knowing what I was doing, and I got caught in the rope of the pulleys. I started to panic. That's almost never happened to me before. I broke out in a sweat. All I wanted to do was to get out of there, but the more I struggled, the more I got tangled up.

"Are you okay?" Patrick asked me. He sounded like he was mad at me.

The blood was rushing to my head.

I felt like a fly caught in a web.

"I'll lower you down, just don't jerk around," said Patrick. "I don't want you to hurt yourself."

"I assume this is a demonstration of what not

to do," shouted Becky. She started laughing. I hated the sound of Becky's laugh.

My right foot was still stuck, so I had to be lowered upside down, dangling from the harness.

Finally, I flopped down on the bed of the trampoline and got my foot untangled. I started to take off the harness.

"Not so fast," said Patrick. "It's like the old adage about the horse. You've got to get right back on."

"I'm not trying out to be a cowgirl," I said. I was still breathing hard, and I don't think Patrick realized that there was no way I was going to get back into that contraption.

"You could be a Bronco Cowgirl," said Chris. The Bronco Cowgirls are the cheerleaders for my dad's team. They are all very beautiful, and actually they are great dancers and acrobats in their own right. Still, I didn't like Chris's snide crack that all I was good for was to cheer on the sidelines — just because I had made a fool of myself in the harness.

I glared at him.

"What did I say wrong?" Chris asked. "I meant it as a compliment."

"Darlene," said Patrick. "Put the harness back on, and we'll try again."

"No!" I shouted at him. "I *hate* that harness. I'm *not* going to put it back on."

Patrick stared at me, a perplexed look on his face. I had almost never refused to do something before.

"I want to try it," said Ashley. "You said that I could be next."

"Here," I said, shoving the harness at her. "It's all yours."

"Darlene," said Patrick.

"I'm sorry, Patrick, but no way — don't make me."

Ashley was tugging at the harness. "Please give me a chance," she said.

"Okay, Darlene, maybe it was my fault for making you do that in front of everybody. We'll try again another day when not so many people are watching," said Patrick.

What Patrick didn't realize was that he could pay me a million dollars but I was not getting into the harness again. As far as I was concerned, that harness was a booby trap.

6

Big Beef's Daugher

I was finished for the day and glad of it. I was heading for the locker room when I felt a hand on my arm.

It was Chris. I wondered what he wanted. I remembered his crack about the Bronco Cowgirls. I was sure that he was just another boy who thought it was *so cool* that my dad was a football player. Boys were always impressed with my dad. When I was a little kid I had to watch out for boys who liked me just because of him. It started as early as kindergarten. Boys would invite me to their birthday parties, and they wouldn't invite my friends. And then I'd find out why.

"I could give you a few hints about using the

trampoline," said Chris. "I saw that you had trouble with it. The first time I used it, I got all tangled up, just like you did."

"I *hate* that contraption," I said.

"You've got to come down straight when you're in the harness," said Chris. "Just think of the trampoline as having a bull's-eye, and you want your toes to hit the bull's-eye every time. Soon it gets so you don't even have to look for it."

"It won't work for me," I said.

"Oh, it will," said Chris.

"You don't understand," I said. "I'm not getting into that thing again. I don't need any help."

It was so obvious that Chris was just trying to be nice to me because of my dad. I pushed open the door to the locker room.

I felt someone sidle up to me.

"Nice going, Darlene," said Becky.

"Look, Becky, I've already had enough humiliation for one day," I said. "I don't need any more."

"I wasn't talking about humiliation," said Becky. "I meant it as a compliment. You were the one who said you weren't interested in Chris, yet you played the little helpless one so well that you got all his attention. Don't think I'm not watching you!"

"Becky, go climb into a harness somewhere," I said.

Lauren giggled. "Becky's jealous," she whispered. "She can tell that Chris likes you."

"He doesn't like me," I objected.

"He does, too," said Lauren. "I'm rooting for you."

"This isn't something you root for, Lauren," I said.

"Sure it is," said Lauren. "Don't you know? We've got a bet going. Becky's friends said that he'd invite her out first. We said that it would be you. We made the bet the day he arrived. I'm sure we're going to win our bet."

"You bet on who he's going to date first?" I practically shouted at her.

"Shh!" said Lauren, giggling. "I wasn't supposed to tell you."

Jodi overheard us. "Oh, Lauren, you didn't spill the beans, did you?"

"It just slipped out," said Lauren. "Besides, it's not nice to keep secrets from Darlene. Maybe Chris already asked her out. I saw them talking outside the locker room. She's got to do it for the honor of the Pinecones."

"Darlene probably has so many dates she can't keep them straight," said Ti An.

"Ti An," I said, exasperated. "I've never had a date."

"*You've* never had a date?" exclaimed Lauren.

"No," I admitted. "And I'll be darned if my first

date is going to be to win a bet for you guys."

"Don't be mad at us," pleaded Cindi. "It was a stupid thing to do. But you can still go out with Chris, can't you?"

"I'm not going out with that creep just for the honor of the Pinecones," I said.

"Why do you call him a creep?" asked Jodi. "He's been nice to you. He's been nice to all of us, but I think he likes you the best. He's always watching you and waiting for a chance to talk to you."

"Oh, yeah? Did you hear his crack about my being a Denver Bronco Cowgirl?"

"I thought it was a compliment," said Lauren.

"Wrong on two accounts," I said. "I don't want anyone to think of me as a Denver Bronco cheerleader."

"You dressed up as one for Halloween," Jodi reminded me.

"That was different," I said. "I *chose* it. Somebody just didn't assume that was all I could be."

"I don't think that's what Chris meant," said Lauren. "I think you're taking this a little more seriously than he meant it."

"I am not. And besides, he's obviously got Bronco-mania on the brain."

"One comment," said Jodi. "That's all he said. It's you who's going on and on about the Broncos."

35

"Why are you making such a big deal if you don't like him?" asked Lauren.

"I think Darlene's just in a bad mood 'cause she had such trouble with the harness," said Ashley.

"Darlene will figure it out," said Cindi.

It was easy enough for her to say. Cindi had done very well on the harness. She was practicing full twists, something she can't possibly do without the harness. Everybody seemed to get the hang of it except me. I felt like such a klutz.

Ti An took to it as if she had been using one all her life. She was by far the most natural on the trampoline, getting incredible height. She did twists and double backs.

I was the only one who seemed to have flunked harness practice. It was humiliating.

I finished changing and headed out of the locker room. Jared and Chris were talking to Becky, but Becky was all but ignoring poor Jared.

"Hi, Jared," I said, coming up to them. Jared gave me a relieved smile.

"Uh, Darlene," said Chris, "Becky was just asking about the trampoline. I was telling her about the bull's-eye idea."

"I thought Darlene was going to stay tangled in the harness forever," said Becky.

"The harness is tricky when you're first using it," said Chris. "When I tried it in the beginning, I think I was more upside down than right side up, most of the time. You know, Darlene, to-morrow, or next week, you'll try the harness again," he said. "It'll be fun. The harness can be your friend."

"You sound like Mr. Rogers from *Mr. Rogers' Neighborhood*," said Jared.

"You don't give up, do you, Chris?" I said.

Chris grinned. He seemed so sure of himself. "No . . ."

"Read my lips, Mr. Rogers — the harness is not going to be my friend," I snapped.

"When Darlene says no, she means no," said Jared. "She can be as stubborn as her dad when he digs in."

"What does Darlene's dad have to do with any-thing?" asked Chris.

"Don't you know who Darlene's dad is?" asked Jared.

Chris shook his head. I stared at him. Was he playing a game with me, trying to act innocent?"

"Her dad's Big Beef Broderick, that's all!" said Jared. "Don't tell me you haven't heard of him."

"Your dad's Big Beef?" exclaimed Chris. "You've got to be kidding. Wait till *my* dad hears that I've met Big Beef's daughter!"

Suddenly I felt terribly embarrassed. I was mad at Jared and mad at myself. I had been mean to Chris because I thought he knew already — and he didn't. He wasn't acting before. He was just trying to be nice and helpful. But now he *did* know. And it changed everything.

Have You Ever Wanted to Strangle Your Dad?

On Friday when we finished our cool-down, Patrick said, "Remember, girls, I want you to write down your private thoughts on your strengths and weaknesses this weekend. Don't worry about grammar or spelling or even spend too much time on it. I just want you to tell me where you think you can improve."

"Darlene can improve on her manners to Chris," teased Ashley.

I glared at her. I guess I had been a little bit rude to Chris all week. I just found talking to him really awkward. It seemed easier to avoid it altogether.

"Ashley," warned Patrick, "don't stick your nose into other people's business."

Ashley giggled. "Patrick doesn't know about our bet," she whispered to me.

"It's a good thing," I whispered back. "He wouldn't like it any more than I do."

"I heard Ryan tell Jared that he thinks Chris likes you," whispered Cindi.

I hated the fact that the gym was turning into a place where all the Pinecones did nothing but gossip about me. I didn't know what to do about it. It wasn't exactly the kind of problem that I could go to Patrick about. It was just too embarrassing.

I went into the locker room and stripped off my leotard. I pulled on a clean pair of tights and put on my sweatshirt. I shoved my towel and leotard into my gym bag and started to take off.

"Hold it, Darlene," said Cindi.

"I can't wait," I said impatiently. "What do you want?"

Cindi started to giggle. I put my hands on my hips. "What's so funny?" I asked.

"Sorry," said Cindi, "but look at yourself. You can't go out like that."

I looked down. My sweatshirt was inside out and backwards. "I don't care," I said.

"Darlene not care how she looks?" bellowed Becky. "I think hanging upside down in that harness earlier this week must have affected her brain. No wonder she hasn't dared go up in it again."

"Very funny, Becky." It was a weak response, but it was all I could think of. I grabbed my gym bag and headed out the door. Cindi stopped me. "Darlene, are you okay?" she asked.

"You sound just like Becky," I retorted. "Please leave me alone."

"It's not like you to go around with a sweatshirt inside out."

I felt really hurt. "Is that what you think of me? Some vain kid who only cares about how she looks?"

Cindi looked hurt. "No. . . . I'm the one who's always messy. Today you look more like me."

"I don't think she even showered," said Lauren.

"What's the matter, Pinecones? Are you worried that you'll lose your bet?" I asked.

"I told you she'd be mad if she found out," said Ti An, sounding worried.

Becky laughed. "Darlene, you've got the most to lose."

"Becky, as far as I'm concerned you can marry Chris," I said. "I don't want anything to do with him. The bet is called off."

Jodi looked upset. "Darlene, we're sorry. We were just fooling around, and Becky was bragging that Chris liked *her*, not you. Becky, we officially call off the bet."

"That's fine with me," said Becky. "I knew Chris would have better taste than to ask out a Pinecone." She strutted out the door.

"We don't want you to go out with Chris if you don't like him," said Cindi.

"She likes him," said Lauren. "I know it."

"Will you guys just drop it, please?" I was fed up. I shoved open the locker room door and practically knocked Chris and Jared over. They were standing right outside.

"What do *you* two want?" I demanded.

"Uh . . ." Jared started stammering, which isn't like him. "Ryan told us that your dad's outside," he said. "He's waiting for you. I told Chris we could go up and talk to him. But he didn't want to. He said we had to ask you."

"Sure," I muttered.

"Look," said Chris, "I don't want to bother your dad."

"Big Beef's terrific," said Jared. "I've talked to him lots of times, haven't I, Darlene?"

"Oh, yes," I said. Suddenly I wondered if Jared had been nice to me all along just because of my dad. It hadn't seemed so before, but now all he cared about was showing off in front of Chris how well he knew Big Beef.

"Darlene's dad comes to all her meets during

the off-season," gushed Jared. "You can't miss him. He makes Patrick look like a midget. And he's even gotten us tickets to the Broncos games. You don't have to be embarrassed to meet him."

"*I'm* not embarrassed," said Chris. "I just don't want to embarrass Darlene."

I looked at him closely. Boy, this guy was smooth. He knew just how to pretend to say the right things to make me think that he wasn't that interested in my dad. What a liar!

"You're not embarrassing me," I lied myself. "I'm sure Dad would love to meet you. Come on!"

"See, I told you," I heard Jared whisper to Chris. "You were wrong. Darlene isn't hung up on people liking her just because of her dad."

I turned around just in time to see Chris poke Jared sharply with his elbow.

"Ouch!" exclaimed Jared.

We walked out to the parking lot. Dad was sitting in the Bronco station wagon.

"Shoot," said Jared. "I was hoping he'd be driving the maroon Corvette. It's the coolest car."

"He fits better in the Bronco," I said. "It's more comfortable."

"And it's more fitting," joked Chris.

"Huh?" I said. I didn't get it.

"A Bronco in a Bronco," said Chris. "It sounds like a great ad."

"It already *is* an ad, dodo," said Jared. "Don't you know anything?"

Chris blushed. "I don't watch much TV," he said. "I don't have much time with all the training I have to do for skiing and keeping up with my homework. Nobody gets to watch much TV in my house."

"Well, at least you watch football games, don't you?" asked Jared.

"Yeah," said Chris. "Well . . . sometimes."

Dad waved to us. He got out of the car. I'm so used to dad, I have no idea what it's like to meet him for the first time. To me, he looks almost normal-size when he's not in all his padding for his football uniform. The uniform and helmet make him look like a giant. He's not. He's six-feet-five, and he weighs 245 pounds. Dad is an offensive lineman, which means that his biggest job is to protect the quarterback. He has to be quick on his feet, and he's even caught a pass once or twice in a surprise play. Dad's got such quick reflexes that he can catch a fly with his bare hands. He says that he always knew he could move quicker than his friends. When he was little he dreamed about being a basketball player. Instead of just growing tall, he grew bigger and bigger. Not fat, just big. Kids started calling him Big Beef when he was little, even though my grandmother, Geebee, has always hated that nickname. She still hates it. I don't like it, either.

Chris looked up at my father.

"Awesome, right?" said Jared. I could have choked him.

"Hi, honey," said Dad. "How're you doing, Jared?"

"See, he knows my name," whispered Jared.

"Fine, Mr. Broderick," said Jared. Dad was no longer paying any attention to Jared. He was staring at me. "Darlene," he said, "are you okay?"

"Yes," I said. I threw my gym bag into the back of the car. Dad was still staring at me. "Your sweatshirt is on backwards."

I gave Dad a dirty look. I shrugged. "I know," I said.

"You do?" asked Dad. "Does this mean you want me to stop on the way home so you can buy a new one?"

"I don't need a new sweatshirt, Dad," I said. "Don't talk about my sweatshirt, okay? There's somebody who wants to meet you."

I opened the car door and sat in the front seat. "Dad, meet Chris Ferguson. He's a fan."

Chris held out his hand. "Actually, my dad's the one who is a huge Bronco fan," he said.

Dad laughed. "And not you?" he asked.

Chris blushed. "No, no, me, too. . . ."

"Chris is a great athlete, too, Mr. Broderick," said Jared. "He's Olympic caliber."

"Really, as a gymnast?" asked Dad. "That's quite a coup for Patrick."

"No," said Chris quickly. "It's my sister who's bound for the Olympics. I'm not a gymnast. I'm a skier, and I'm not nearly fast enough for the Olympics. But I started doing freestyle skiing. It's not an Olympic event yet."

"Not that stuff where you do somersaults in the air — with skis on. That's incredible!" exclaimed Dad. "You must have nerves of steel."

"Uh-uh," said Chris.

"It's going to be an exhibition sport at the Winter Olympics. Chris might be on the team," bragged Jared.

"That's a big might," said Chris modestly. "It's my sister who's the sure thing for the Olympics."

"You sound like quite an amazing family," said Dad. "Does your sister work out with Patrick?"

"Dad," I complained. "She's too good to work out with us."

"Well, it's not that . . ." stammered Chris.

"Dad," I interrupted. "Don't we have to go home?"

"Oh, right," said Dad. "Chris, it was nice to meet you. If you ever are doing some of that freestyle skiing when I've got some time off, let me know. I'd love to watch it."

46

"That would be great, sir," said Chris. "I'd love it if both you and Darlene could come."

"It would be a treat," said Dad. Dad looked at me. "Wouldn't it, Darlene?"

"Oh, sure," I muttered. I rolled up my window.

Dad climbed in and started the car. "What's wrong with you?" he said as soon as we were alone. Sometimes I feel like strangling my dad. It was exactly the wrong kind of question to ask me.

8

First Fight

"Well?" repeated Dad. I wrapped my arms around my chest and hugged my forearms.

"Well, what?"

"Chris seems like a very nice boy. Why were you so mean to him?"

"Mean? Me?"

"You," said Dad. "You wouldn't look at the poor guy, and all he could do was look at you."

"Very funny, Dad. You're the one he's impressed with. I don't want to talk about him."

"Sorry," said Dad. He chortled. I hate it when Dad chortles — it's more like a giggle. The guys on his team are always teasing him about his laugh. It sounds like it comes from a comic book. He almost goes, "Tee . . . hee . . . hee." It's as funny-sounding as the way he sneezes Dad is the only person I know whose sneeze a sounds like "Ah choo!"

"Tee hee hee, yourself," I said. We pulled up front of the house. I grabbed my gym bag from the back and slammed the door shut.

"Watch it, young lady," said Dad. "I don't mind that you're in a bad mood, but don't take it out on my car door."

"I'm not in a bad mood," I said. I walked through the garage into our kitchen. I grunted hello to my Mom and went up to my room and closed my door.

I realized I had to write that silly essay for Patrick on my strengths and weaknesses.

I turned on my computer. The blinking cursor on the screen was pulsing at me like a nagging teacher. I wondered what Chris would write down for his strengths and weaknesses. *Great athlete — good-looking — I come from a family where everyone goes to the Olympics.*

What should I write down? *Good-looking — I come from a family where everyone expects me to be a great athlete, except I'm not.*

I typed into the computer the words: *I follow directions well. I listen to my coach.* Those things were true, but they sounded like such nerdy traits.

Usually writing comes easily to me, but not

today. I got up from my desk and wandered around my room. I reread an old *Elle* magazine. I looked at a *Baby-sitters Club* book that I had already read three times. Maybe I would just go see Patrick and tell him that I had nothing interesting to write about myself. I opened a biography of Amelia Earhart that I had used for a book report three months ago. Maybe I should try to become an astronaut like Jodi's sister, except that I hate math and science. I was getting really desperate.

The cursor on my screen was still blinking at me. I sighed. I wished my phone would ring. Mom and Dad got me my own telephone line on my birthday. They said that as a teenager I would need my own phone. Mom and Dad made a much bigger deal of my becoming a "teenager" than I did. I don't feel that much older or different than I did at twelve. It's as if everybody expected me to change into something else just because my age added the silly word "teen."

My little sisters are way younger than me. Debi is only four, and Deirdre is fourteen months old. The TV reporters don't expect an active player to have a teenage daughter, and they make a big deal out of me. I'm older than most of the other kids of the players on the Broncos.

I have to admit that I do like having my own phone line, even though it kind of embarrassed me at first because none of my friends has her own line. It is nice that I don't have to wait for Mom and Dad to get off the phone when I want to talk.

I wished that something would happen so that I wouldn't have to write. Maybe I would call Cindi or Jodi. It didn't seem fair that we should have to write for gymnastics.

I put my hand out for the phone, and I felt the vibration as it rang as if by magic.

"Saved by the bell," I said. I was sure it was one of the Pinecones.

"Wow!" said a voice. "You must have been sitting on the phone." The person on the phone sounded strange, almost as if he were trying to disguise his voice.

"Practically," I admitted. I didn't recognize the voice. It sounded like someone with a stuffy nose. "Who is this?"

"It's Chris," he said, and his voice cracked. I'm glad that girls' voices don't change. It must be very weird to hear your own voice go up an octave when you least expect it. "Jared gave me your number. I hope you don't mind."

"It's okay," I said, wondering why he called.

"Uh . . . well, how are you?" Chris asked.

"I'm fine," I said. "I just saw you a half hour ago. Nothing much's changed."

The cursor on my machine was still blinking

as if to remind me that I wasn't quite telling the truth. What had changed was that when I tried to write about myself I had come up with an enormous case of writer's block. Even a phone call from Chris, probably wanting to know if Dad could get him tickets for a game, was a welcome relief.

"I . . . uh . . ." Chris was stammering. I decided I would make things easier for him.

"You want to know if Dad can get you tickets for the Bronco game." I finished his sentence for him.

"Oh . . . do you mean he could really do that?" asked Chris.

I sighed. I *knew* that was why Chris had called.

"Probably," I said. "Dad liked you. He doesn't get too many tickets, but I know he's planning on taking Cindi and her brothers to the next home game in two weeks. He invited the other Pinecones, and I could see if he could get you a ticket."

"Uh, thanks," said Chris in a rush. "I never expected that . . . I mean . . . my dad won't believe it."

"Great," I said. "Glad to be of service. I'll let you know in the gym. 'Bye — "

"Hey, wait, Darlene," Chris said quickly as I was about to hang up the phone.

"What?" I asked.

"I called to see if, uh . . . maybe you wanted to go out," said Chris. "They've got this great new indoor miniature golf course that's opened right near the mall. I thought, maybe if you liked miniature golf, maybe we could try it."

I thought that if he added another "maybe" I'd scream. "I'm not very good at miniature golf," I said.

"That's okay," teased Chris. "There're no harnesses to get caught up in. . . . We can play just for fun."

"You don't have to ask me out just because I'm getting you a ticket," I blurted out.

"Uh . . . I didn't. In fact, I didn't call to ask for a ticket. I called to ask for a date."

"Oh, sure," I said, a little sarcastically. "I find that hard to believe."

"Why would I lie?" Chris asked.

"Oh, please, Chris. Don't you think I'm used to guys wanting to get to meet my father? I can spot them a mile away."

"Well, you'd better get new glasses," said Chris. "I think you've got a vision problem . . . and a personality problem."

"And what exactly does that mean?" I asked him.

" 'Mean'!" Chris's voice cracked. "*You're* the one who's mean."

"Mean? Me?" I exclaimed. "I think you must

have dialed the wrong number. I'm sure you meant to ask Becky out and to say that to her."

"I didn't think I had the wrong number," said Chris. "But maybe you're right. You don't give anybody a chance. You make up your mind, and you're just so sure that you're right. Maybe I should have called Becky."

"Why don't you hang up right now and call her?" I said.

"Why don't you stop bossing people around?" said Chris.

"Thank you very much," I said. "Patrick's asked us to write about our strengths and weaknesses. You've made it easy for me. I can write that I'm mean and bossy. In fact, I've got to get back and write that right now. Good-bye."

I slammed down the phone. *I* had a personality problem? He was the one with the personality problem. Somehow we had managed to have our first fight, and we hadn't even had a first date.

9

Game of Revenge

I rolled my chair back to the computer. I was not going to let the things that Chris had said upset me. He was just a stupid boy. He didn't know anything about me.

My favorite event is beam, I wrote, *because it forces me to concentrate. My strengths are that I can concentrate, and I'm not sloppy. My second favorite event is floor because I like to dance. I don't like vault or the bars. I don't like to take risks that mean I'm going to fall off.*

I looked at my computer. Patrick had said that this wasn't an assignment. I didn't have to write any more. I started to save it and turn off my computer.

I stared at the phone, mad as heck. How dare

Chris tell me that I was mean and bossy! I'd show him.

I added a line for Patrick. *My greatest strength is that I'm nice to my friends and my teammates. I never boss them around.* Then I printed it out and saved it. I clicked off the computer, and pushed my chair away from the desk so fast that I hit the wall behind me.

I knocked myself into my bookshelf and the top books come tumbling down on top of me. "DARN IT!" I yelled.

Dad came running into the room. Debi peered at me from behind his legs. "What happened?" he asked. I rubbed the top of my head.

"Nothing!" I muttered at him. I pushed past Dad and went to the kitchen. Dad followed me. Mom was cutting up vegetables for soup. I grabbed a carrot stick.

"Darlene said a dirty word," tattled Deirdre.

"I did not," I said, munching loudly.

"What are you in such a sulk about?" Mom asked.

"I'm not in a sulk. I'm a very nice person."

Mom and Dad stared at each other. "Who said you weren't nice?" Dad asked me. He looked angry. It's the kind of look that makes the players on the opposite team get very worried.

"Chris Ferguson," I said.

"That boy we just met?" Dad exclaimed. "You're kidding!"

"I'm not," I said.

"Darlene, why did he say that to you?" asked Mom, sounding a little suspicious. I was a little sorry that I had told them about it.

"Just because I wouldn't go on a date with him," I said.

"He said that to you because you turned him down!" asked Dad. "That boy needs to be taught some manners."

"Wait a minute, both of you," said Mom. "Darlene, I think something's missing here. What exactly happened?"

"He just likes me because of Dad," I said.

"How do you know that?" asked Mom.

I shrugged. "I just do. That's all *any* boy is interested in me for."

Mom sighed. "Honey, you have to live with the fact that people will be a little bit in awe of your dad. That's just life. But you've always been able to sort out true friends from fake ones. It's like knowing the difference between the Pinecones and girls like Becky. You just have to trust yourself. Now, maybe you're right about this boy, but not about *all* boys."

I grabbed another carrot stick. Mom was making me uncomfortable. She was being too rational. I wasn't in the mood for rationality.

"Darlene," asked Mom, "how do you know that you didn't just jump to the conclusion that he liked you only because of Dad?"

"I told you, I didn't jump to conclusions. And I'm being very nice to him. I want Dad to get him and his father tickets to the game, anyhow," I said. "Can you do that?"

Dad stared at me. "Why would you want me to get a ticket for somebody who just put you down? I don't want you to have anything to do with the fellow."

Mom smiled at me. "Maybe there's something more going on here than we know," she said.

"Mom!" I protested. "You're as bad as the Pine-cones. I don't like Chris Ferguson. And I *know* he doesn't like me. I just want to prove to him that I'm better than he thinks. When I show up and give him a pair of tickets, he won't believe how *nice* I can be. I'm just going to show him up, that's all."

"Why do you care so much?" Mom asked.

"Because Chris Ferguson thinks he knows it all," I said. "He's a great athlete. His sister is heading for the Olympics. He is, too. Everything comes *so* easy for him."

"That's what a lot of people say about you," said Mom. "And you know that's not true. Maybe you should give this boy a second chance."

"No way. He's probably already asked Becky out. The Pinecones are going to be disappointed that they lost their bet, but who cares?"

"The Pinecones had a bet on which of you this boy was going to ask out?" Dad asked. "This is getting weirder and weirder. And you still want me to get tickets for this creep for the game?"

"And for all the Pinecones," I said.

"Darlene, do you know what you're doing?" Dad asked.

"I think Darlene's mighty confused," said Mom.

"Thank you very much," I said.

"On the other hand," said Mom, "I don't think you'd be half this upset if you didn't like him."

"Mom! You're sounding exactly like the Pinecones. And wipe that grin off your face. I don't need my mother grinning at me," I told her.

"Sorry," said Mom. "It's your business. Dad and I shouldn't interfere."

"Thanks," I sniffed. I looked at Mom for signs of sarcasm. I hate it when Mom or Dad are sarcastic, but Mom at least sounded as if she meant it, that it was my business and not theirs. "I just want Dad to get tickets for Chris," I pleaded. "That'll prove to him that I'm a nice person."

"You've always been a nice person," argued Dad. "You don't have to prove it to anybody."

"I think she does," said Mom. "Just do what

she says, Eric. Darlene knows exactly what she's doing."

Mom winked at me. I knew what she was thinking. She thought that I really liked Chris and that I was playing some kind of game. She couldn't have been more wrong.

The only game I was playing was one of revenge. I'd teach him to call me *mean* and *bossy*. I'd be so nice, so disgustingly sweet, he'd be very sorry.

The Zen of Coaching

Chris, Jared, and Ryan were talking to Patrick when I walked into the gym with the Pinecones. They were looking at us. We started our warm-ups. I sat on the mats and twisted my wrists around to warm them up. Then I stretched my arms behind me. Cindi stood in back of me. I put my arms on her shoulders, and she pulled slowly. It's an exercise that we do to stretch out our shoulder sockets so that we can do the giant turns on the uneven bars.

Becky walked by. "I say, Darlene. Are you holding up your arms in surrender?"

Cindi groaned. "Becky, can't you ever walk by without a nasty crack?" Cindi was so mad that she pulled extra hard on my arms.

"Ouch!" I exclaimed.

"Sorry," she muttered.

"I'm not at all in a nasty mood today," said Becky with a big smile on her face. "I'm in the best mood ever. I just wanted to tell you Pinecones that you lost your bet."

"We told you, Becky," said Jodi. "The bet is off. We were stupid to make it, and we don't care who Chris asks out."

"You're just saying that because you lost," sneered Becky.

"I never made a bet with you, Becky," I reminded her. "Have a good time playing miniature golf."

Becky did a double take. "Who's talking about miniature golf?"

"Didn't Chris ask you to play miniature golf?" I asked her.

Becky frowned. "Uh . . . no," she said. "He asked me to go watch him do a freestyle ski competition this weekend. That's much more personal. Miniature golf is goofy. Why would you think somebody like Chris would want to play miniature golf?"

"Because last night he asked me to play miniature golf." I couldn't resist bragging.

"All right!" said Cindi. "Sorry, Becky, but Darlene got the date first."

"I'm not going," I said.

Becky smirked. "See," she said. She didn't look quite as happy, however, as when she first announced that she had a date. She lay down on the mats across the room from us and started her own warm-ups.

Cindi dropped my arms and came around in front of me. "Chris asked you out, and you turned him down?" she said. "Why?"

I shrugged.

"Are you still mad at us because we made that bet with Becky?" asked Jodi. "Because that's no reason not to go out with him. We already apologized for making that bet. And we called it off. It's not our fault that Becky has to keep up her meow act."

"Shhh," I warned Jodi, as I watched Patrick and the boys' team come over to us.

"Girls," said Patrick, "Chris here asked me to say something to you."

Jodi poked me. "Maybe he complained to Patrick about you turning him down," she whispered.

"That's not funny," I hissed. It really wasn't. I would die of embarrassment.

"Chris," said Patrick, turning to him, "why don't you ask them?"

Chris blushed. He shook his head.

"Is this something that's going to get us out of doing gymnastics today?" asked Ashley.

"No," said Patrick. "This is a treat for all of us. There's going to be a freestyle competition at Breckenridge this weekend, and Chris has invited everybody at the gym to come watch him. We're going to rent a bus so that all the teams can go."

"Becky's team, too?" asked Cindi. "Did you invite Becky?"

"Cindi, I said *all* the teams," said Patrick. "Chris and I just told Becky's team about it a few minutes ago."

Ti An started to giggle. "So that was Becky's big date," whispered Ti An.

"Uh, your dad said he wanted to watch a freestyle competition," mumbled Chris without meeting my eyes. "Will you tell him about it?"

"He's got an away game this weekend," I said.

"It's going to be so neat," said Jared. "Chris said that we can get seats right next to the jump. We'll be able to see the fear in their eyes."

"It'll be scary enough just watching those jumps," cooed Ashley. She sounded like a miniature Becky.

I stood up, pretending that I was going to do some more stretches.

"Oh, by the way, Chris, my dad was able to get you Bronco tickets for the weekend after next."

"All right!" exclaimed Jared. "That's the same weekend that we're going!"

"And all the Pinecones," said Cindi.

"Two weekend treats right in a row," said Jodi. "What could be better?"

"Nothing," muttered Chris. "Right, Darlene?"

"Uh, right," I said.

"Okay, boys and girls," said Patrick. "Let's get back to practice. We've got plenty of work to do."

Patrick got out his clipboard. "I'd like everybody to turn in their list of strengths and weaknesses," he said. "Then continue your warmups."

We handed them in.

"I *hated* doing that, didn't you?" said Jodi. "Everyone knows that I like the bars the best. I hate the vault."

"I'm the opposite," said Lauren. "It's no secret that I like the vault."

Patrick quickly glanced through our sheets. "Okay, girls, thank you," he said. "I know that wasn't easy, but it makes my work easy for today. Darlene, you'll be working on the vault. I want you to master a handspring with a full twist."

"Wait a minute!" I exclaimed. "You said to tell you our strengths and weaknesses. Vault is my weakest event."

"Exactly," said Patrick. "That's the point."

"Is this supposed to be some kind of new Zen coaching?" asked Jodi.

"You've got it," said Patrick. "While I'm working on Darlene's vault, I want the rest of you Pinecones to work on the first half of the floor exercise. Cindi, you lead them."

"Because I hate dance, right?" muttered Cindi.

Patrick just smiled at her. I watched the other Pinecones troop off behind Cindi. "Okay, Darlene," said Patrick. "Let's go over the specific techniques for the vault."

He drew a diagram of a girl twisting to her right as she did the handspring on the vault. "You'll have to remember to keep your right arm close to your body," he said, as if mastering this vault would be a simple matter.

"Patrick" — I looked up at him — "I think this vault is too advanced for me."

He shook his head. "You're wrong, Darlene. You've been stuck in the water for a while now. It's time to take a leap forward. You're ready for some risks."

"How do you know?" I asked him.

"It's your age. You're a teenager. Teens thrive on risks, and gymnastics is the perfect place for it."

"I'm not just some typical teenager," I argued.

"I know that," said Patrick.

"I'm not my father, either," I said.

Patrick put his hand on my shoulder. "Darlene, this is me, Patrick. I've never been guilty of that confusion. You know that."

I nodded. He was telling the truth. I absolutely knew that Patrick didn't like me because of my father. Patrick cared for me for myself.

"You can't keep hiding behind your father," said Patrick.

"I don't do that," I argued.

Patrick smiled at me. "Then get into the harness and start learning the twist for the new vault."

"Patrick, me and the harness are not going to work."

"The harness and I," corrected Patrick.

"We're not being graded on grammar. I'm not kidding, Patrick. I'll try to learn the vault, but I don't want to use the harness. I'll do anything not to do it."

"You won't be able to master this new vault unless you can safely practice it on the harness."

"The harness is too scary for me!" I protested. "You can't make me use it."

Patrick looked puzzled. "I'm not going to force you, but, Darlene, I've never asked you to do something that you weren't ready for."

I looked at the harness contraption. All I could think of was the humiliation of hanging upside down from it.

"No!" I said defiantly.

11

Is That a Fact?

I was in a terrible mood all week. Patrick didn't insist on my using the harness. I could tell that he kept thinking that I would come around by myself. I felt like a chicken for refusing. Yet feeling like a chicken was *not* enough to make me try it again.

I kept circling it whenever I was practicing.

Patrick caught me staring at the harness. "You know, Darlene, the only way to conquer fear is to do it, even though you're afraid."

"Oh, boy, the old 'get back on the horse after it's thrown you' cliché," I said.

"Often clichés are true."

"I can't do it, Patrick. I'll do anything you say, but not that."

"Okay," he said. "We'll try the vault without the harness. I'll spot you."

Patrick stood at the end of the vault, and I tried doing the handspring, but every time I tried to twist in the air, I didn't have enough height. I couldn't even get a quarter of the way around.

I tried it three times, and I was exhausted. "It's not working," I admitted. "I just think that vault's too hard for me."

Patrick pumped himself up onto the vault and sat on it. "It wouldn't be if you would practice it in the harness," he said.

I sighed. I couldn't think of a really good excuse why I was being so stubborn. I just knew that dangling up there, out of control, was something that I did not want to do.

Patrick slipped off the vault. "Come with me, Darlene," he said.

We walked over to the trampoline and harness. "I know I'm being silly," I whispered. "I just can't do it."

Just then Chris came over. "Can I use it next, Patrick?" he asked. "I've really got to practice before the exhibition this weekend. But I'll wait until you finish with Darlene."

No way was I going to try the harness again with Chris watching. I shook my head. "I'm not using it," I said.

"It's all yours," said Patrick.

"You're going to come out to Breckenridge, aren't you?" asked Chris. He sounded as if it mattered to him whether I came out to see him or not.

"I think so," I said.

"I really want to show you what I can do," he said.

Becky walked by. She had an uncanny ability to find Chris no matter what else she was supposed to be doing.

"Chris, I can't wait to see the freestyle competition," she said. "I'm going to be so nervous for you."

"You don't have to be," said Chris. "It's a lot less dangerous than regular skiing. Fewer people get hurt. It just *looks* dangerous."

"Oh, you're just being modest," simpered Becky.

"No, I'm not," said Chris. "Nobody would ever accuse me of being modest."

He jumped up onto the trampoline and put on the harness. Patrick adjusted the pulleys. Chris made it look *so* easy. I remembered watching him the first day and thinking that I would get the hang of it right away.

"He's so smooth," I heard a voice behind me say. Jared was looking up at Chris.

"Yeah, almost too smooth," I said.

Jared looked surprised. "You know, I thought

that when I first met him. I thought Chris was stuck-up, just because he's so good, but he's not like that at all."

"You like him?" I asked.

Jared nodded. "Say, Darlene," he said. "Chris has been talking."

I steeled myself. If Chris has been gossiping about asking me out and my hanging up on him, I would kill him. I didn't care how good an athlete he was.

"About what?" I asked Jared.

"Well, Chris says that we guys should go easy on you, asking you for tickets for the Broncos games. He says that it can't be easy being the daughter of a big star. I just didn't want you to think we were being pushy, asking for tickets."

"I don't," I said. Chris did a double back and then floated down to the trampoline as if he were weightless.

"You know," said Jared, "it's pretty ironic. Chris says that his father's a big football nut, but Chris doesn't really know the game at all. He says he never had time to watch football 'cause he was always training so hard."

"Is that a fact?" I asked Jared.

12

Why Did I Care
So Much?

The air was so cold that it hurt to breathe. It was the coldest day of the year. It was just the beginning of December. I couldn't believe that we had three more months of this cold. I cupped my mittened hand over my mouth to warm the air before it got to my lungs, the way that my dad does on a really cold day when he has to play football.

I was wearing my one-piece bright orange ski suit that's supposed to keep me warm in subzero temperatures. It wasn't subzero. It was officially ten degrees out, but the wind-chill factor was minus twenty.

The entire Evergreen Gymnastics Academy was huddled around a real evergreen tree, trying to stand as close together as we could in order to keep warm. Chris wasn't scheduled to begin his competition for an hour. He had guided us over to the side of the ski-jump area and told us where to stand. He was dressed in a one-piece bright red speed suit. He wore a blue parka over it, and he carried a helmet. The helmet reminded us all of what he was about to do.

I stamped my feet and looked up at the smaller of the three ski jumps. I couldn't believe that Chris was going to deliberately go off it, turn in the air, and then attempt to land right-side up.

"Aren't you worried about killing yourself?" Lauren asked, which was exactly what I was thinking.

"Killing myself is the least of my worries," joked Chris. "I'm worried about making a fool of myself. I'm sorry it's so cold. Are you all going to be okay?"

"Don't worry about us," I said. Chris and I really hadn't exchanged any private words since the moment I had hung up on him. Now, standing outside looking up at the ski jump, I felt a little sorry for him. It couldn't have been easy inviting us all to come see him.

"Are you nervous?" I asked.

"Yeah, I've never had so many friends watching me at one time before," he said.

"You'd better get used to it," said a girl standing next to him. "It never gets easier."

I looked at her. She was one of the palest girls I had ever seen, and thin. She had black hair, which only made her look even paler. She wore aviator sunglasses that covered most of her face. And she clung to Chris as if she were made of Velcro. I wondered if she was a girl from his school. Becky was staring at the girl, looking jealous.

I stamped my feet some more to try to keep warm.

"Chris," said the girl, "you'd better get ready and get with your coach."

"I know," said Chris. "But I want to introduce you to my new friends at the gym. . . ."

"Never mind," said the girl, interrupting him. "I can take care of myself. Don't worry about me."

Chris did look worried, more worried than he did about the competition.

"Uh . . . okay," he stammered. He left quickly.

The girl watched him go. She seemed to be relieved. She wrapped her arms around herself. We were all standing like that, trying to keep warm, but she looked different, as if she were holding herself tight so that nobody would get to her.

I didn't know whether to talk to her or not. Finally I decided that it was silly to be standing next to her and not to introduce myself.

I stuck out a mittened hand. "Hi, I'm Darlene Broderick," I said.

The girl shook my hand. She muttered something, but her voice was so quiet it got lost in the wind.

"Excuse me," I said. "I didn't catch your name."

"It's Heidi Ferguson," she said.

"You're Chris's sister. The gymnast," I said. "I can't tell you what a thrill it is to meet you."

"Chris has told me about you, too," she said. She didn't make it sound like it was much of a compliment.

"I thought you were in California at the Supertwisters Gym," I said.

Heidi half turned her back to me. "I'm here to watch my brother, not to talk about gymnastics, okay?" She tried to smile, but it was a tight smile. Maybe I had insulted her or something.

Jodi came to stand next to me. "Is she Chris's girlfriend?" she whispered.

I shook my head. "His sister," I said.

"The gymnast!" exclaimed Jodi.

"Let's not tell Becky that she's his sister," whispered Cindi. "I like to watch Becky get jealous."

I laughed, but a little uncomfortably. I had felt a little twinge of jealousy myself when I thought Heidi was a girlfriend of Chris's from school.

We stood around watching the regular ski

jumpers soar through the air off the big jump.

"I can't imagine having the nerve to do that," I said. Heidi heard me.

"They all start just like we did in gymnastics," she said. "They start with real little jumps, and the only ones who keep going are those who *want* to. To them it's natural — like doing back flips is for us."

I didn't want to admit that doing back flips *wasn't* the most natural move for me. "Do you get nervous watching Chris?" I asked.

She shook her head. "Naw, my parents do. They can't watch either of us at a competition. It makes them too nervous. They used to want to come to watch me, but it made *me* nervous worrying about *them* being nervous, so I don't let them come."

"Does Chris come to watch your meets?"

Heidi shook her head. "I don't want *anybody* from my family watching me," she said.

That was pretty definite. I wondered what she was doing out here. As it got closer and closer to the time for Chris to make his jump, I was the one who got really nervous for him. I had to ask myself, why did I care so much?

13

Risk and Adventure

"Hey, kids!" shouted Patrick. He pointed up the ski jump. "I think that's Chris."

"Who's that?" Heidi whispered to me. "Is he the coach that Chris told me about?"

"That's Patrick," I said. "He's terrific."

"That's what Chris says," said Heidi.

"Do you want to meet him?" I asked.

Heidi nodded her head shyly. It was strange to think of a great gymnast being shy about meeting a coach.

I introduced Heidi. Patrick smiled at her. "Pleased to meet you," he said. Patrick turned his attention back to the ski jump. Heidi seemed relieved that Patrick didn't make a big deal over her.

"Chris is going to be the first," he said.

I looked up at the smaller of the ski jumps. There was no elevator. The jumpers had to climb stairs next to the jump, holding their skis on their shoulders.

I could make out Chris in his bright red ski suit. He stopped about two thirds of the way up the stairs and put on his skis. Then he waited.

"The waiting's always the hardest," said Heidi.

"Always," agreed Patrick. I imagined Patrick was thinking of his own waiting before competitions, but maybe he was thinking of the times as a coach where he has to wait to see how each of us do. The waiting for Patrick must be almost worse than it is for us.

"Right now Chris's stomach is doing more flip-flops than he's going to do in the air," said Heidi. "I know."

Chris started to slip sideways onto the jump. He wasn't using any poles. He adjusted his goggles and looked down the jump, out across the landing run-off, forty feet above the lip of the jump.

Someone must have signaled him that the judges were ready. Suddenly he pointed his skis down the jump. He gathered speed. His hands were close to his body, but as he got to the lip of the jump, he spread his arms wide, exactly like a bird soaring. Then he brought his arms over his head, the way a gymnast would if he were doing a flip, and he flipped backward. His long skis clattered against each other as he fought to control the flip. Imagine doing a flip with six-feet-long sticks strapped to your feet. He came out of the first flip, still twisting, and he tucked his chin to try to get around for the second.

"Pull!" Heidi shouted at him. Chris had to bend his knees. The ground was rushing up at him. If he didn't hurry, he was going to land on his head. He veered to the side, and his left ski hit the ground first. He must have been going about sixty miles an hour. He got his right ski down and managed to keep his balance in a crouched position. Finally he stood up and slowed himself down at the end of the run.

I let the air into my lungs. I didn't realize that I had been holding my breath.

I looked at Heidi. She let out a deep sigh. "He's not going to be happy with that one," she said.

"I thought it was incredible, until the very end," I said.

"Yeah, but he's not going to win with that landing. You watch — the other guys are better than he is. Chris has *got* to really steam on his second jump."

Patrick was clapping his mittened hands together and shouting at Chris. "Way to go, Chris!" he yelled.

"It wasn't a very good jump," said Heidi.

Patrick was grinning. "Look, it's an adventure just to be out there doing that stuff," he said. "I think your brother is magnificent."

Heidi looked at Patrick as if he were from outer space.

"But I told you," said Heidi, "that was a lousy jump."

Patrick shrugged. "He'll get better. I've got faith in Chris."

"He's *not* going to win, you know," she said.

"I'm not so sure about that," said Patrick.

"There're other skiers who are just better than he is," insisted Heidi. "It's not Chris's fault, but he's not the best."

"Maybe he won't win today," said Patrick. "Still, Chris has got something special. In the long run, he'll be a winner."

"Do you mean . . . he's a nice person?" asked Heidi sarcastically. "Everybody always says that my brother is nice."

"I do think he's nice," said Patrick, "but that's not what I was talking about."

Heidi turned her back on Patrick and shielded her eyes from the sun. I took a step closer to Patrick. I thought about what he had said about risk and adventure. Maybe that's what was missing in my life.

Patrick looked down at me. He was smiling. "What did you think?" he asked.

"I thought Chris was pretty terrific," I admitted.

"I did, too," said Patrick.

"He's not afraid of taking risks," I said.

Patrick didn't answer me for a minute. "I'd like to see you put a little more risk and adventure into your gymnastics," he said. "You can learn a lot from Chris."

We watched the other jumpers. I had to admit that most of them scored higher than Chris. When Chris had invited us to come watch, he hadn't put himself down — he hadn't made any excuses like, "Hey, don't expect me to win or anything." I admired him for that.

"Oh, look," said Patrick. "Chris is going to do his second jump."

"He'd better pull it out," said Heidi.

I crossed my fingers inside my mittens. I really wanted Chris to do well.

Chris sped down the ski jump and flew into the air. This time he managed to keep his legs straight through the second flip!

"He's got it!" I shouted.

"Now hit the landing!" shouted Heidi, and she was grinning. Suddenly she looked a lot younger and a lot nicer. Heidi grabbed my arm.

We watched as Chris straightened himself out. He seemed to be in the perfect position for a great landing, but as his skis hit the snow, he lost his balance. He went crashing into the fence, right by our feet.

Heidi's grip tightened on my arm. We stared down at Chris, who was all tangled up in his skis.

"Is he okay?" asked Lauren. "I couldn't look."

Chris got up a little wobbly. Then he took off his goggles and waved.

"He's fine," I said to Heidi.

"Yeah," she said, "but he screwed up."

I stared at her. It wasn't the screwing up that counted; it was the fact that he had even risked it at all.

14

It's Easier
on the Phone

Chris didn't come close to winning. He ended up fifteenth out of twenty-five.

"Not even in the top half," said Heidi, as she rushed over to the sidelines to talk to him. I wanted to follow her, but I didn't feel as if I had the right.

I wanted to tell him that I thought he was good, even though he had fallen on his landing. Heidi was talking to him very intently, and I didn't want to intrude.

All too soon it was time for us to get on the bus. I had a window seat next to Jodi for the ride home.

Jodi kept hugging herself trying to keep warm.

"It makes you appreciate gymnastics," she said. "At least we do it inside."

I laughed, but I wasn't really concentrating on Jodi's words.

"I thought Chris was terrific, even though he didn't win," said Lauren. "I like the way he really came through on his second jump."

"Wasn't it exciting meeting Heidi Ferguson?" gushed Ashley. "To think we actually got to meet someone who is probably going to the Olympics!"

"I read where she's our only real medal hope," said Ti An. "She didn't seem particularly cheery."

"Cheery?" said Lauren. "I thought she was downright depressing. She seemed to think that Chris had let everybody down by not winning. I wouldn't want her as my sister."

"We didn't talk to her very much," I said. "I don't think we know what she's like."

"Well, I didn't like her," said Lauren, positively.

I was the one who used to brag that my first impressions were always accurate. I wasn't so sure anymore.

I kept thinking about Patrick, talking about risk and adventure. Heidi wasn't afraid of risk and adventure. She was taking her talent to the limit and so was Chris. It was I who was stuck, always comfortable to be just in the middle where it was safe.

It was already dark out. I stared out the window into the blackness.

When I got home, Mom wanted to know all about the ski jumping. I didn't feel like talking. I ate a quick dinner, went to my room, and sat down to do my homework. I was having a hard time concentrating.

I kept staring at the phone, thinking about Chris. I couldn't get him out of my mind.

Finally I picked up the receiver, and I punched in his number. A girl answered the phone.

"It's Darlene," I said. "Is this Heidi?" For some reason this time my voice cracked, and I had to fight to get it back down.

"Right," said Heidi. Her voice sounded flat, as if she remembered me, but she wasn't too happy about it. I decided to try to make friends anyhow.

"Did you thaw out?" I asked.

"I'm still frozen through," she said.

"I bet you'll be happy to get back to California," I said.

There was a pause on her end of the phone. "I'll go get Chris," she said.

I stared at the receiver and fiddled with my hair. Maybe I shouldn't have called, but it was too late to hang up. Chris already would know it was me.

I took a deep breath.

"Hello," said Chris.

"It's Darlene," I said. "I just wanted to say that I thought you were great out on the jump. I was really glad that I got a chance to see you perform." I sounded like such a total jerk.

"Uh, thanks." Chris sounded a little surprised that I had called, and I couldn't blame him.

"Are you sore after your fall?" I asked.

"Yeah," said Chris, "but that goes with the territory. I was really glad that you came."

"Me, too," I admitted.

"Did the other Pinecones like it?" Chris asked.

"Lauren refused to look. She couldn't stand it when you fell. But we all thought you were great. We didn't care whether you won or not." I paused.

"Yeah, well, *I* do," said Chris.

"Your sister cares, too," I said.

"Don't hold that against her," Chris answered.

"I don't," I said. "I admire it."

"She's kind of having a hard time right now," said Chris, "but she said she liked meeting you. She said that you and your friends seemed to like each other."

"Did that surprise her?" I asked.

"A little," Chris admitted. Then he giggled. I liked the fact that Chris giggled. It reminded me that he was just thirteen, too.

"What are you laughing at?" I asked.

"I don't know," he said. "Do you realize that you and I have talked more on the phone than we have in person? Let's not fight this time."

"I didn't call to fight," I said. I thought about asking Chris if his invitation to play miniature golf was still open, but the words stuck in my mouth.

So Chris and I talked a little more about freestyle skiing and a little more about gymnastics, and then we hung up and I still didn't know what was going on.

But I felt a lot better about it all.

 *15*

Once Isn't Enough

I went to gymnastics on Monday with a feeling of excitement that felt great. I wasn't just in a good mood; I was in a *super* mood. I put on a brand-new one-piece leotard with pink and purple stripes going every which way. It was really jazzy.

"You look cheery," said Cindi when she saw me.

"Thanks," I said.

"What put you in a such a good mood?" asked Lauren.

I shrugged.

"I know," teased Jodi. "This Sunday we're all going to the Broncos game, and Chris is going. It'll be their first date."

"Chris is not my date," I said. "There's a big bunch of us going. Besides, I'm just in the mood for gymnastics."

"It's a proven fact that you can go out with somebody cute *and* be a good gymnast," said Lauren.

"Where did you read that, in *Dear Abby*?" I asked. Lauren always says that something is a "proven fact," and she often has an obscure source for her facts.

"I just made that one up," said Lauren, "but I know it's true."

"Well, I'm not going out with him," I said. "So you can stop fantasizing about it."

"Well, you *are* going to the football game, aren't you?" asked Cindi.

"Yes," I said.

"And he's going to the football game," said Cindi.

"But it's not a date," I said.

"What's not a date?" asked Becky.

"Nothing," I said.

"Chris and Darlene do not have a date for the football game," said Lauren.

"Who cares?"

"I thought you liked Chris," I said.

"Chris . . . he's too juvenile," said Becky.

"Maybe you didn't like that he didn't win yesterday," I said.

"I say Becky didn't like that Chris didn't pay any attention to her," said Cindi.

"You Pinecones are so immature," said Becky. "Darlene, consider the bet off."

"It was off long ago," said Cindi indignantly. "We told you it was off about a dozen times."

"Well, now I'm officially calling it off. You have my permission to go out with him," said Becky.

Somehow that cracked up all the Pinecones. We were laughing so hard that Becky stomped out of the locker room.

"I like *her* giving you permission!" said Cindi.

"Well, I didn't like you betting on my social life — especially before I even had one," I said.

"We know that, Darlene," said Lauren with a sigh. "We'll mind our own business from now on." I looked at her a little skeptically.

"Okay, okay," she admitted. "We probably won't mind our own business, but we'll try. Okay?"

"Okay," I said. "Let's remember what Patrick said about gymnastics instead of gossip."

After I finished my warm-ups, I went up to Patrick. I took a deep breath. "I'm ready to try the harness," I said.

"Great," said Patrick. "I was hoping you'd come around. What made you change your mind?"

"Seeing Chris do his flips from the ski jump.

If he can do that, I can learn to use the harness."

"The harness is just the beginning," said Patrick. "Wait till you learn to try the trick without the harness."

"One step at a time," I said.

"You're right," he said. "Let's get started."

He pulled down the harness. I climbed into it and started my jumps.

"Now, remember," said Patrick. "You'll be turning so fast that you won't be able to spot anything outside of your body. Don't even think about the outside world. You want to be looking for your right shoulder as you do the twist. That will force you around."

"What if I get tangled in the wires again?" I asked.

"You'll just have to get untangled," said Patrick.

"That sounds like good advice," I said.

Becky walked up to us. "I need time on the harness today," she announced.

"After Darlene's finished, you'll have a turn," said Patrick. "Darlene's starting to learn a vault with a full twist."

"You've got to be kidding," said Becky. "Darlene? That vault is over her head."

I tested the harness and started jumping up and down. I looked down. Chris was standing near the trampoline, looking up at me.

Patrick had said to blot out the entire world. I tried. Patrick pulled down on the pulleys. It made staying in the air effortless. I threw my legs over my head and twisted to the right, keeping my eyes focused on my right shoulder.

I tried to tune out everything that was below me — Becky, Chris, the rest of the Pinecones. I had to concentrate just on myself, on me twisting around myself.

I was scared that I would panic again. All I was worried about was getting through it, but to my complete surprise, it was fun. I did a complete twist so high in the air I felt like I was flying, and I didn't tangle the wires. Patrick kept the pressure just right. I would never have believed that I could have done that move. It wasn't a safe move — it was a risky one.

I pointed my toes back toward the trampoline and came down right in the middle. I heard someone shout, "Bull's-eye!" It was Chris.

Slowly my eyes started to focus again. I saw Becky giving Chris a dirty look.

"Thirteen-year-old boys are so infantile," she said loudly.

Then I heard laughter in the background. It was the Pinecones.

I laughed with them. It's hard to laugh in the harness. I hiccupped.

Patrick tugged on the pulleys. "Try it again, Darlene," he said.

"You mean once isn't enough?" I asked.

Patrick shook his head. "It's just the beginning," he said.

16

The Second Date Could Be Fun

It was a cold, nasty day, not quite as bitter as the day of Chris's freestyle competition, but almost. My father hates playing football in the cold. The field becomes a muddy battlefield in the center and a frozen ice rink on the sidelines. The football players slip and slide and feel like they're playing hockey without skates or sticks. I knew Dad would be worrying more about fumbles and interceptions than anything else.

There was a lot of empty seats even though the game was sold out. More than 12,000 ticket holders decided it was a nice day to stay home and watch football on television.

Still, 60,000 of us were bundled up and freezing in the stands. The temperature was eighteen degrees and falling; the wind-chill factor was zero and falling. I felt like I was turning blue.

The Pinecones were laughing and cheering as if it were a summer day. They acted as if they didn't mind the cold. Chris's father had brought a battery-operated blanket. He was up and down so much, yelling at each play, that the blanket kept falling off him. Chris offered it to me.

"I'm okay," I said.

"I'll take it," said Mom, with a grin. "I can't stand it when it gets this cold."

The Broncos were losing. They had already clinched their division title, and this game was just for pride. I knew Dad wanted to win, but it was hard to really get into the game. I looked around the stands at all the empty seats and kind of wished that we all had been smart enough to stay home.

Chris leaned over to me. "Would you like some hot chocolate?" he asked.

I stood up. "I'll go with you," I said. "Maybe moving around a little will keep me warm, and at least the concession stands are out of the wind."

We asked if anybody else wanted to come with us, but everybody else was too into the game.

The snow was falling harder. I almost slipped on the steps. Chris caught me. "No double flips or twists today," he said. "It's a holiday."

We went beneath the stands. I ordered our hot chocolate. I asked the man at the concession stand to put tops on the cups so we could take them back to the stands.

"Let's drink it here," said Chris.

"Don't you want to get back to the game?" I asked.

"Not really," said Chris. "Do you?"

I shook my head no. "I'm happy to be out of the wind."

"Besides," said Chris, "I want to straighten something out with you."

"I think I already know," I said.

"You do? Are you a mind reader?" Chris asked.

I nodded. "I shouldn't have snapped your head off when you asked me out. Maybe I was too quick to think that all you wanted was tickets to the Broncos game."

"Hey," said Chris. "I thought you were kidding when you said you could read my mind, but you did. Usually when people say they know what you're going to say, they get it all wrong."

I took a slow sip of the cocoa. I could feel it go down, and it warmed me all the way through.

Chris took a sip of his own hot chocolate. "What made you change your mind about me?" he asked.

"Your sister and Patrick said that sports were all about risk and adventure. Some boys get all hung up on making my dad a big hero, but I think those guys don't have enough adventure in their own lives. Nobody could say that about you. I watched you jump, and you had plenty of your own adventure."

"Even though I didn't win," said Chris.

"The winning didn't matter. It was the fact that you were doing it," I said.

Chris sighed. "I wish you could talk my sister into feeling like that," he said.

"I kind of liked your sister," I said. "She's a little intense, but she's honest."

"She liked you, too," said Chris. "She said that even though you turned me down for a first date, I should ask you again."

I could feel my face turn hot, and I don't think it was the hot chocolate.

Chris looked at me. "Do you think we could play miniature golf sometime? It's inside, at least."

"It sounds good," I said.

Chris grinned at me. He giggled. "I was so nervous about having a first date. . . . Maybe it's not cool to tell you . . . that you're my first date, or you will be, if we ever go out."

"Me, too!" I said, practically spitting out my cocoa. "I hate the very idea of having a first date."

Chris lifted his cup. "Hey, I've got a great idea. Let's call this our first date and get it over with."

I grinned to myself. I couldn't wait to tell the Pinecones I had a date to play miniature golf with Chris. I knew that they'd all want to tease me about my big first date.

"It's my second date," I'd be able to tell them.

Chris and I walked back to the stands. We heard a huge roar. I looked down at the field. Dad had just made an incredible block. Swivel-hips George, the running back, broke free.

The people in the stands around us went crazy. Chris was cheering, too.

Chris saw me looking at him. "Your dad is incredible," he said.

"Thanks," I said. Usually when people compliment me about Dad it makes me feel uncomfortable. Somehow when Chris did it, it felt okay. Chris knew me as the kid who had been scared stiff of working out on the harness. But I had mastered that fear and taken the risk of learning something new. Compared with that, going out on a first date was easy. Our second date might even be fun.

About the Author

Elizabeth Levy decided that the only way she could write about gymnastics was to try it herself. Besides taking classes, she is involved with a group of young gymnasts near her home in New York City, and enjoys following their progress.

Elizabeth Levy's other Apple Paperbacks are *A Different Twist, The Computer That Said Steal Me*, and all the other books in THE GYMNASTS series.

She likes visiting schools to give talks and meet her readers. Kids love her presentation's opening. Why? "I start with a cartwheel!" says Levy. "At least I try to."

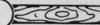